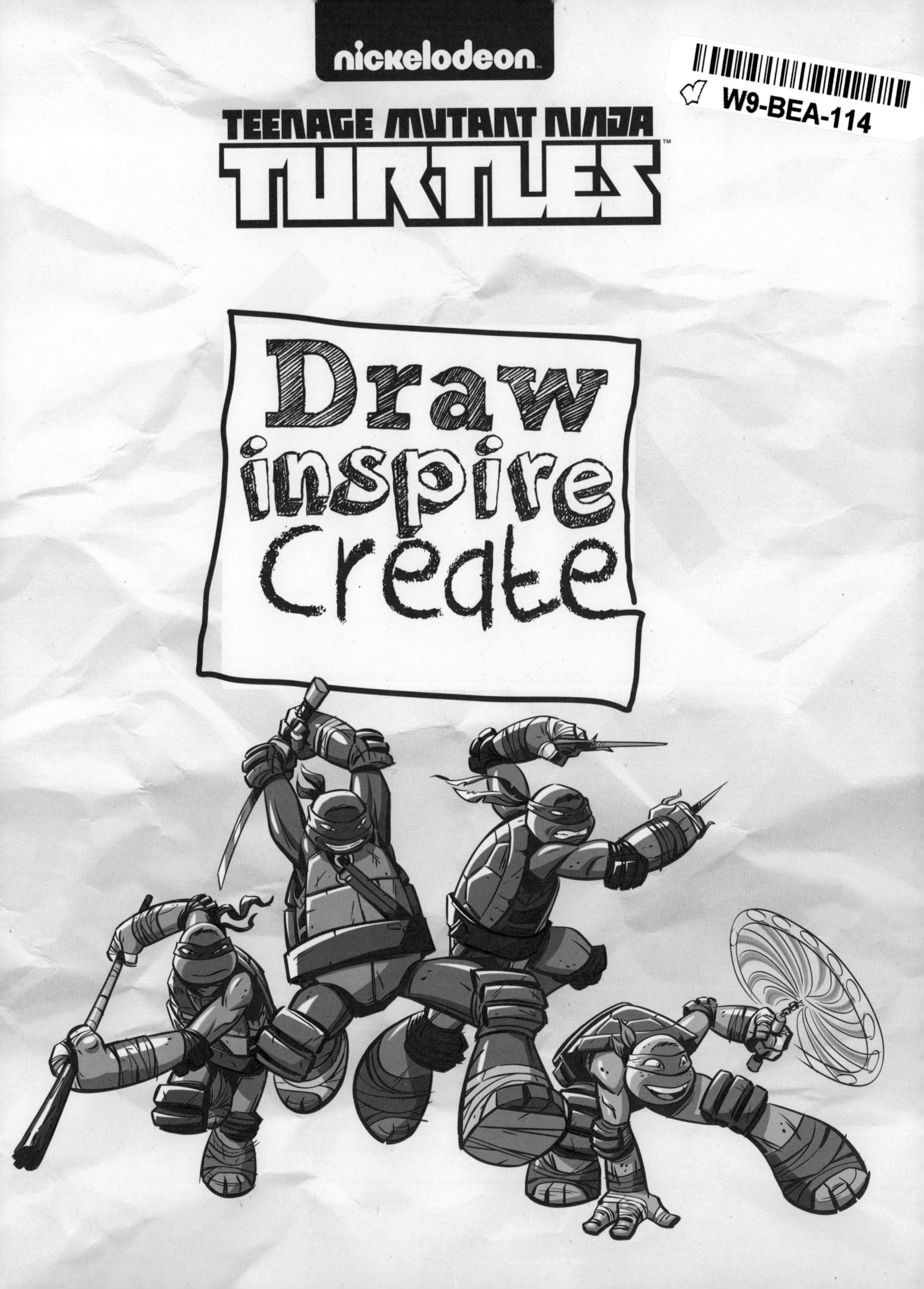
nickelodeon
TEENAGE MUTANT NINJA
TURTLES
Draw
inspire
Create

This BOOK belongs to

....

Write your name here.

This edition published by Parragon Books Ltd in 2014 and distributed by

Parragon Inc.
440 Park Avenue South, 13th Floor
New York, NY 10016
www.parragon.com

ISBN 978-1-4723-4104-4

Printed in China

Draw some
Kraang here!

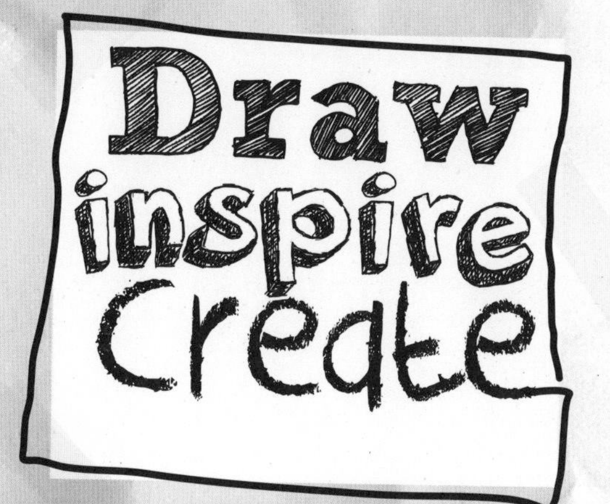

Add an epic scene
behind the Turtles!

Bath • New York • Cologne • Melbourne • Delhi
Hong Kong • Shenzhen • Singapore • Amsterdam

THE TURTLES

LIVE UNDERGOUND IN THE SEWERS.

DESIGN YOUR OWN NINJA ROOM IN THEIR HIDDEN LAIR!

THE DOJO

THE TURTLES' LAIR

APRIL KEEPS A RECORD OF STRANGE THINGS HAPPENING IN TOWN ON HER LAPTOP.

WHAT'S HAPPENED TODAY?

DRAW IT HERE

DRAW AROUND YOUR THUMB
AND FIRST TWO FINGERS.
NOW COLOR THEM IN FOR A . . .

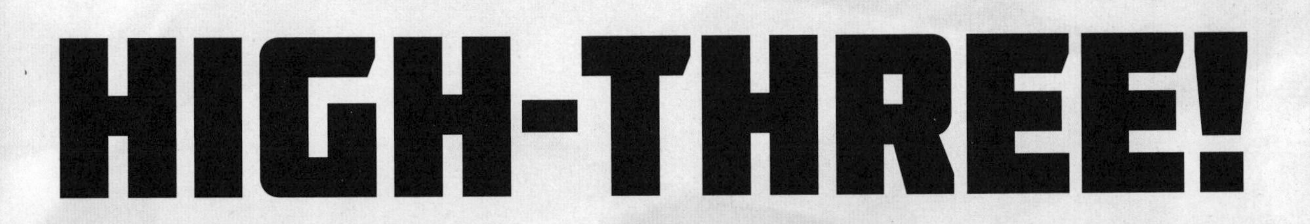

THE TURTLES KNOW HOW TO **TAG TEAM!**

GET THREE FRIENDS AND EACH DRAW PART OF A STORY. THE TITLE IS *TURTLES BASHING BOTS.*

PART ONE

PART TWO

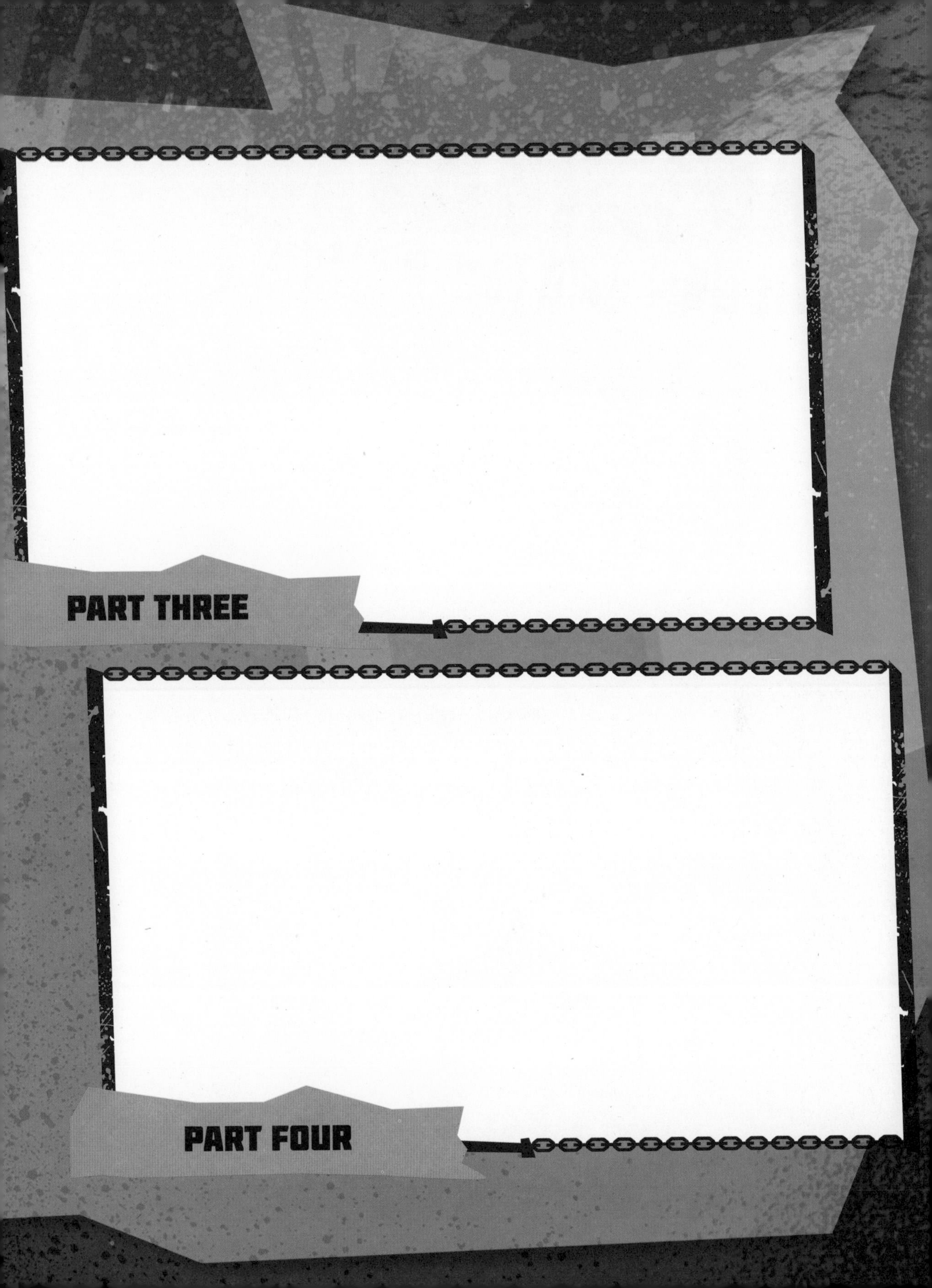

PART THREE
PART FOUR

DESIGN
YOUR OWN TURTLE WEAPON.

MY WEAPON IS NAMED:

....

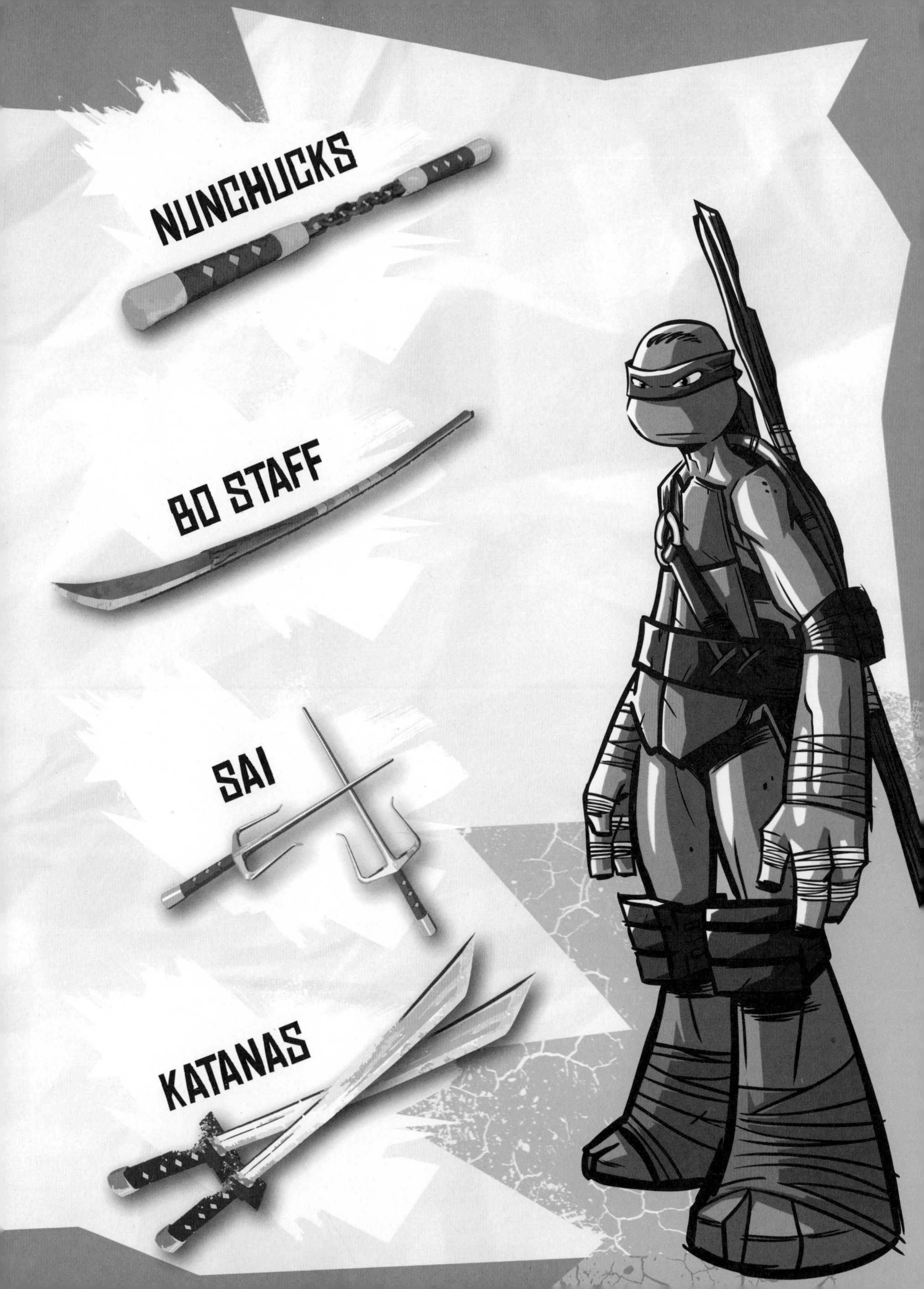
NUNCHUCKS
BO STAFF
SAI
KATANAS

TURTLE
POWER!

WHAT ARE THE TURTLES SAYING? FILL IN THE BUBBLES.

STINKS TO BE THEM!

COLOR IN THE FOOT CLAN
SOLDIER. THEN DRAW A PILE
OF FOOT CLAN SOLDIERS
TAKEN OUT BY THE TURTLES.

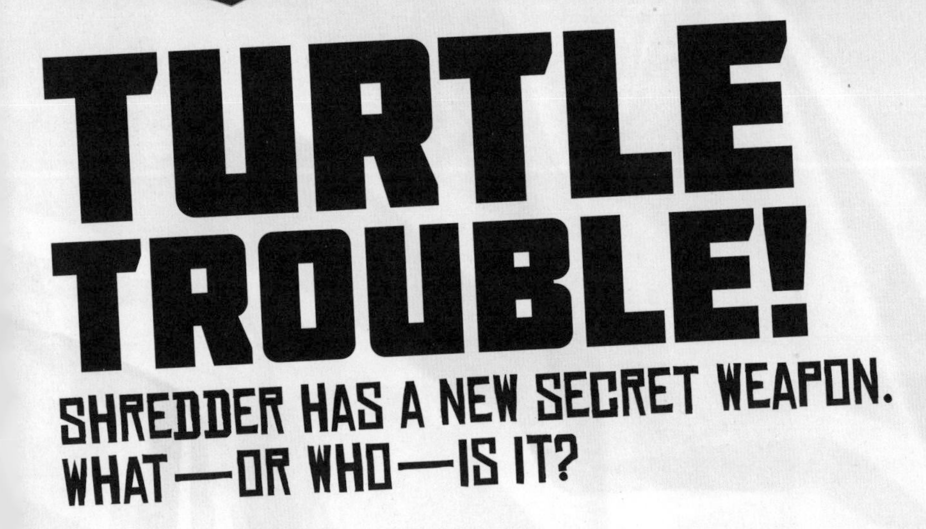
TURTLE TROUBLE!
SHREDDER HAS A NEW SECRET WEAPON. WHAT—OR WHO—IS IT?

BOOYAKASHA!

DRAW A CLOSEUP
OF MICHELANGELO'S FACE
ALL SET FOR GO TIME!

MUTANTS RULE!

TURTLES, RATS . . . WHAT PUMPED-UP CREATURE WOULD YOU MUTATE INTO?

AFTER . . .

THE SHELLRAISER

IS ONE OF DONNIE'S AWESOME INVENTIONS.
ADD SOME MODS AND DESCRIBE WHAT THEY DO!

SHELLRAISER

SPLINTER

IS A RAT-HUMAN HYBRID. DRAW YOURSELF AS AN ANIMAL-HUMAN SUPER MUTANT!

NINJAS IN TRAINING!

SKETCH A SCENE OF THE TURTLES PRACTICING FOR BATTLE.

DONNIE

IS AN EXPERT CODE-CRACKER!

CREATE A CODE BY DRAWING A SIMPLE SYMBOL TO REPRESENT EACH LETTER OF THE ALPHABET.

A	B	C	D	E

F	G	H	I	J	K

L	M	N	O	P	Q

R	S	T	U	V	W	X	Y	Z

PRACTICE YOUR SECRET CODE BY WRITING A MESSAGE:

DESIGN A NEW
KRAANGDROID

THE KRAANG USE KRAANGDROIDS TO GET AROUND. IF YOU COULD DESIGN A NEW ROBOT BODY FOR THEM, WHAT WOULD IT LOOK LIKE?

THE TURTLES LOVE PIZZA! PACK THIS ONE WITH YOUR CHOICE OF AWESOME TOPPINGS.

FISHFACE
HAS CRUSHING ROBOTIC LEGS.
WHAT OTHER DEADLY PARTS WOULD YOU GIVE HIM?

"FREEZE,
SLIMEBALLS!"

DRAW THE KRAANG BRAINS
LEAVING A WEB OF SLIMY TRAILS.

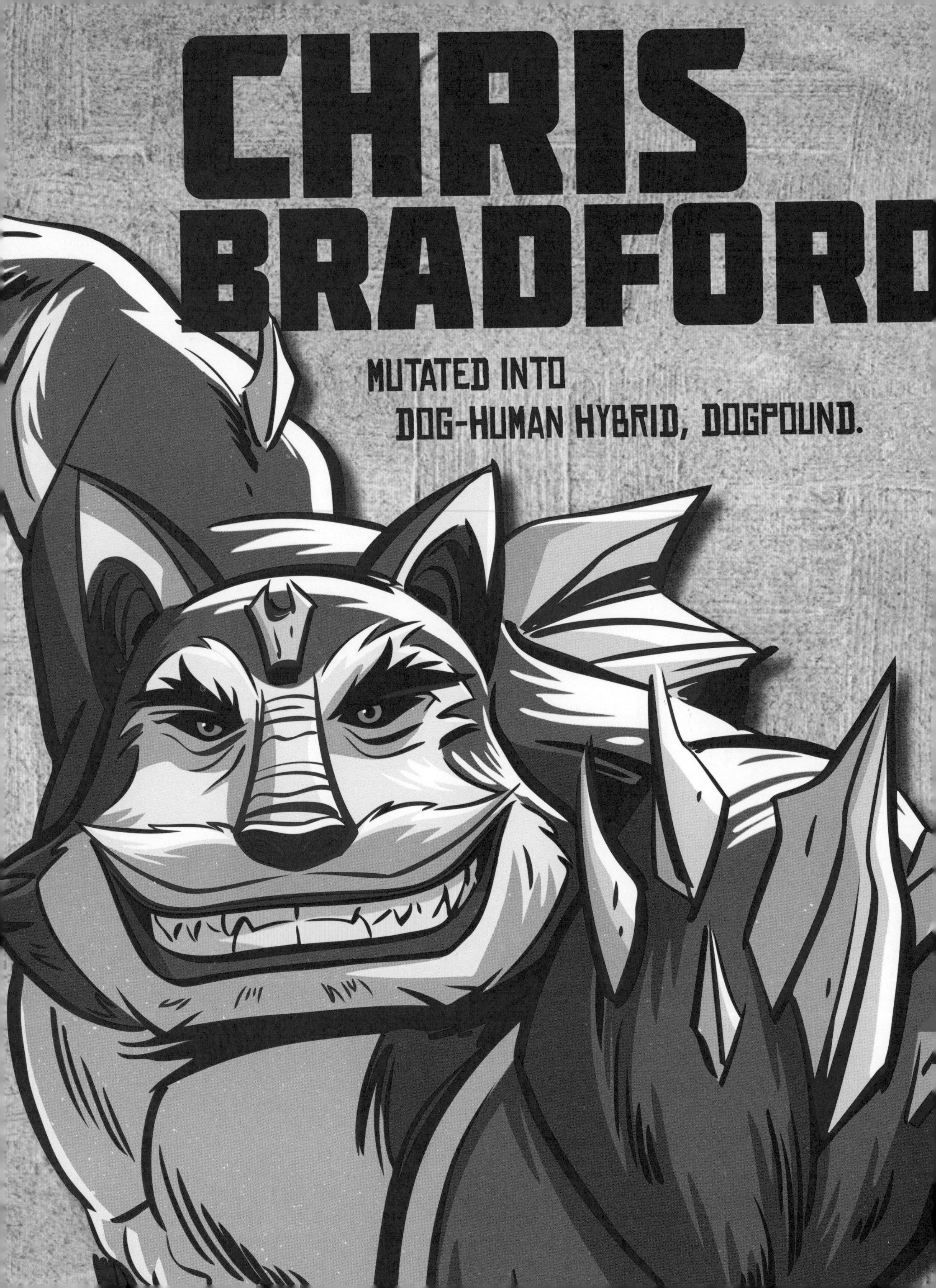
CHRIS
BRADFORD
MUTATED INTO
DOG-HUMAN HYBRID, DOGPOUND.

CREATE YOUR OWN FIERCE DOG MUTANT!

THE KRAANG COME FROM DIMENSION X

WHAT DOES
DIMENSION X
LOOK LIKE?

OK, SHELLBRAIN!

WHAT'S THE FIRST THING THAT POPS INTO YOUR HEAD WHEN YOU THINK OF DONNIE?

DOODLE IT HERE!

SKILLS

WHAT SPECIAL SKILLS WOULD YOU BRING TO THE TURTLE TEAM?

TURTLE NAME: ______________________

WEAPON SKILL: ______________________

SPORTS SKILL: ______________________

BATTLE SKILL: ______________________

LET'S TAKE 'EM DOWN!

DRAW YOURSELF AS A TURTLE HERE!

EVIL SIDEKICK

CREATE A NEW EVIL SIDEKICK FOR SHREDDER—ONE SO BAD THAT SNAKEWEED STARTS TO LOOK LIKE A NICE GUY!

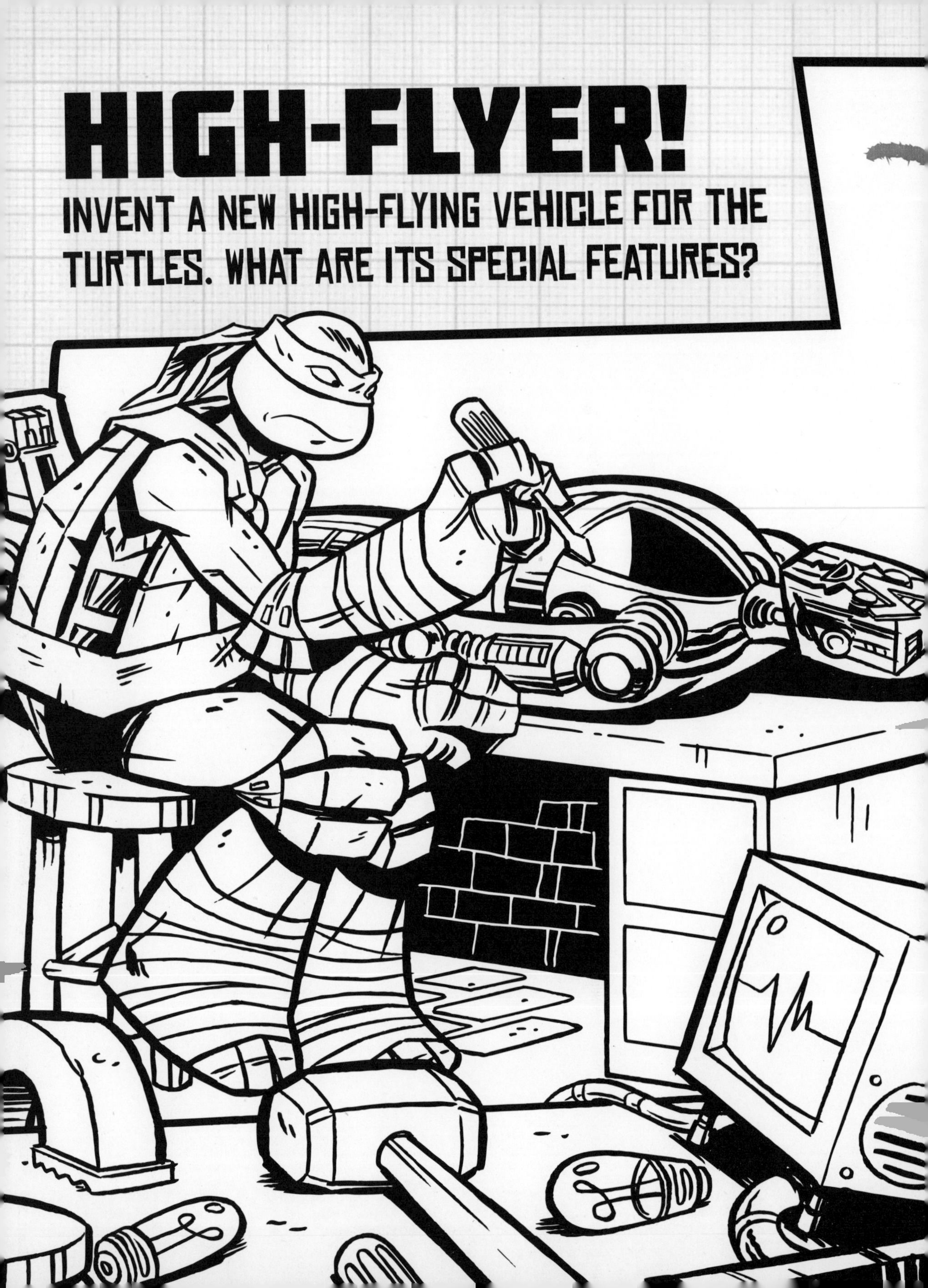
HIGH-FLYER!
INVENT A NEW HIGH-FLYING VEHICLE FOR THE TURTLES. WHAT ARE ITS SPECIAL FEATURES?

JOKES!

RECORD YOUR FAVORITE TURTLE-STYLE JOKES AND COMEBACKS RIGHT HERE!

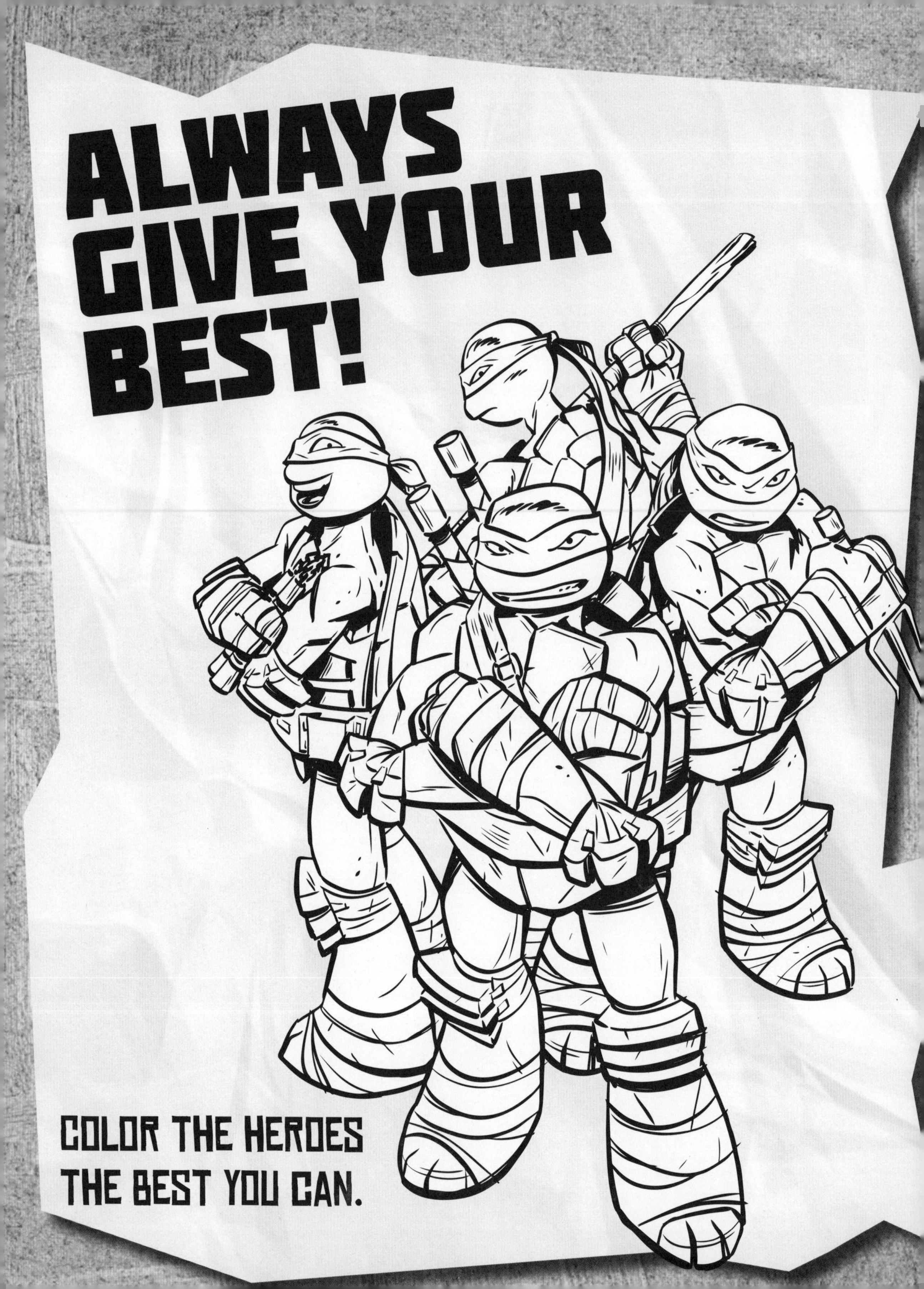
ALWAYS GIVE YOUR BEST!
COLOR THE HEROES THE BEST YOU CAN.

RAPH
IS READY FOR AN ALL-YOU-CAN-BEAT BUFFET!
GIVE HIM AN ARMY OF BOTS TO BASH.

NINJA

THE TURTLES HAVE SOME KICKASS MOVES!

DRAW YOURSELF DOING
A NINJA STUNT.

DONATELLO

HAS CREATED AN UPDATED VERSION OF METALHEAD. DRAW THE NEW ROBOT HERE. WHAT CAN IT DO?

METALHEAD

NEW ROBOT

DRAW A MAP

OF THE TURTLES' UNDERGROUND SEWER NETWORK.

SOMETHING HAS JUST BLOWN MICHELANGELO'S MIN

WHAT IS IT?

WISDOM
COMES FROM EXPERIENCE . . .
. . . AND EXPERIENCE COMES FROM MAKING MISTAKES.

WHAT FIVE THINGS HAVE YOU LEARNED THIS YEAR?

THINK
OF YOUR THREE LEAST FAVORITE ANIMALS. NOW TURN
THEM INTO MUTANT VILLAINS! WHAT ARE THEIR POWERS?

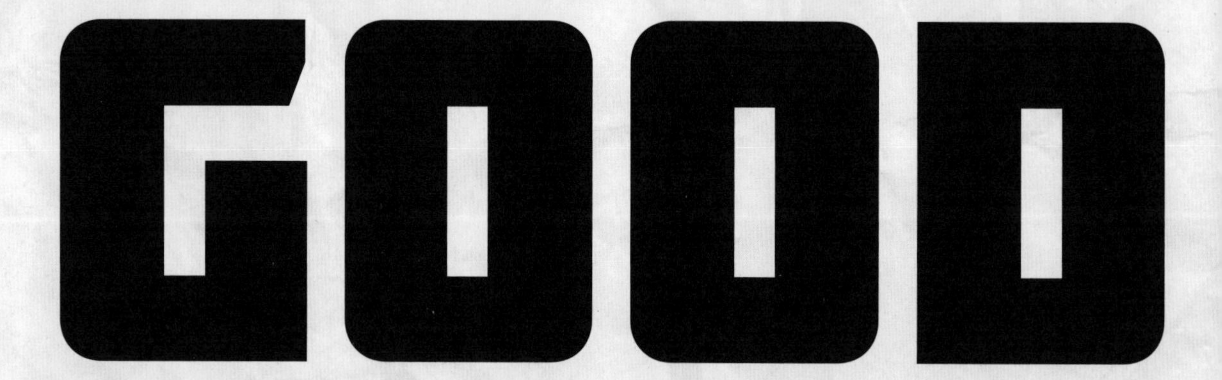

SKETCH THE MOST EPIC THING
THAT'S EVER HAPPENED TO YOU.

TIMES

MIKEY'S
HEAD IS PACKED WITH EPIC IDEAS!
DOODLE WHAT HE'S
THINKING ABOUT.

SPLINTER

TEACHES THE TURTLES ABOUT SELF-IMPROVEMENT.
JOT DOWN THREE THINGS YOU WANT TO DO THIS YEAR.

ANGER
IS SELF-DESTRUCTIVE.

SKETCH FIVE THINGS THAT MAKE YOU MAD!

SHADOWS

A NINJA'S MOST POWERFUL WEAPON IS THE SHADOWS. DRAW YOUR NINJA SHADOW.

DRAW

AROUND YOUR FIST. NOW ADD TENTACLES AND FEATURES TO TURN IT INTO **A KRAANG!**

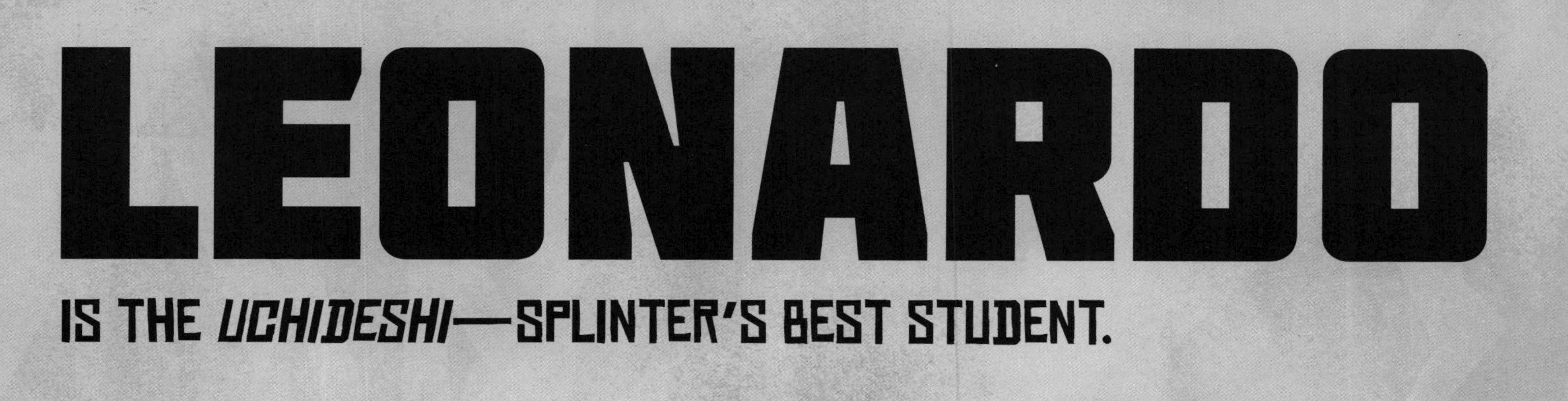

LEONARDO

IS THE *UCHIDESHI*—SPLINTER'S BEST STUDENT.

PROVE YOU'RE A GREAT STUDENT BY DRAWING SPLINTER FROM MEMORY!

SPLINTER SAYS

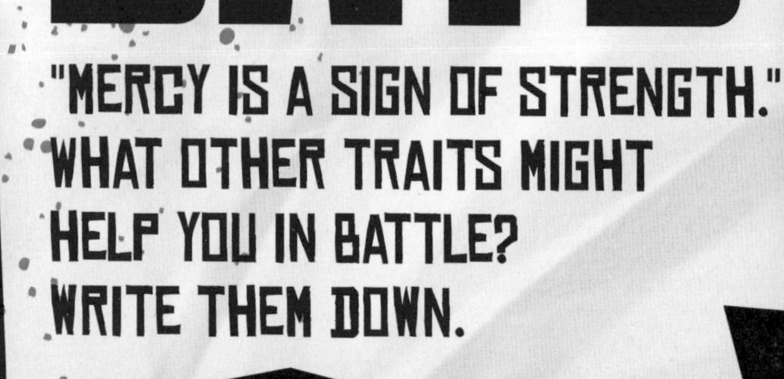

"MERCY IS A SIGN OF STRENGTH."
WHAT OTHER TRAITS MIGHT
HELP YOU IN BATTLE?
WRITE THEM DOWN.

NYC

THE TURTLES LOVE A BIT OF "SURFACE TIME" IN NEW YORK CITY! WHAT'S YOUR FAVORITE PLACE TO VISIT? DRAW IT!

DISH OUT THE
MIGHTY WRATH
OF JUSTICE!

WHO IS LEONARDO FIGHTING?

"WE'RE
SKETCH THE MOST HEROIC ACT YOU CAN THINK OF!

HEROES,

THAT'S WHAT HEROES DO."

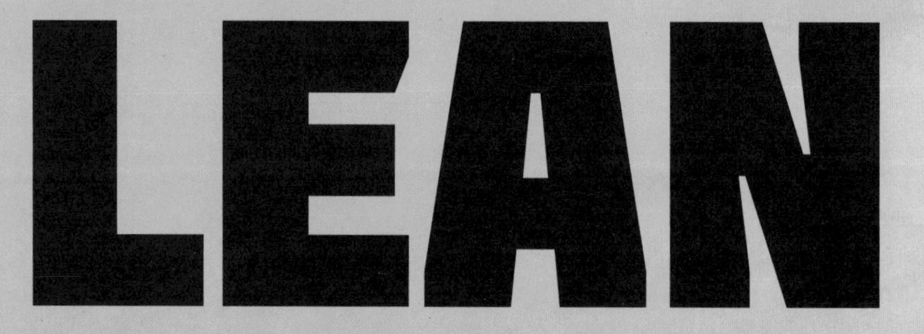

DRAW ALL THE THINGS YOU CAN

THINK OF THAT ARE TURTLE GREEN!

DONNIE

HAS ADDED SOME LASERS TO HIS BO STAFF.

DRAW THE WILD

ZAPS

FLYING

ABOUT!

WANT TO *REALLY* BLOW SOME MINDS?

DRAW AN EXPLOSION!

DONNIE
HAS BEEN WORKING ON A SECRET NEW INVENTION.

WHAT IS IT?

SOME BAD GUY IS SNEAKING UP ON LEO!

WHAT'S YOUR TURTLE CATCHPHRASE?

SCRIBBLE YOUR IDEAS ON THESE PAGES.

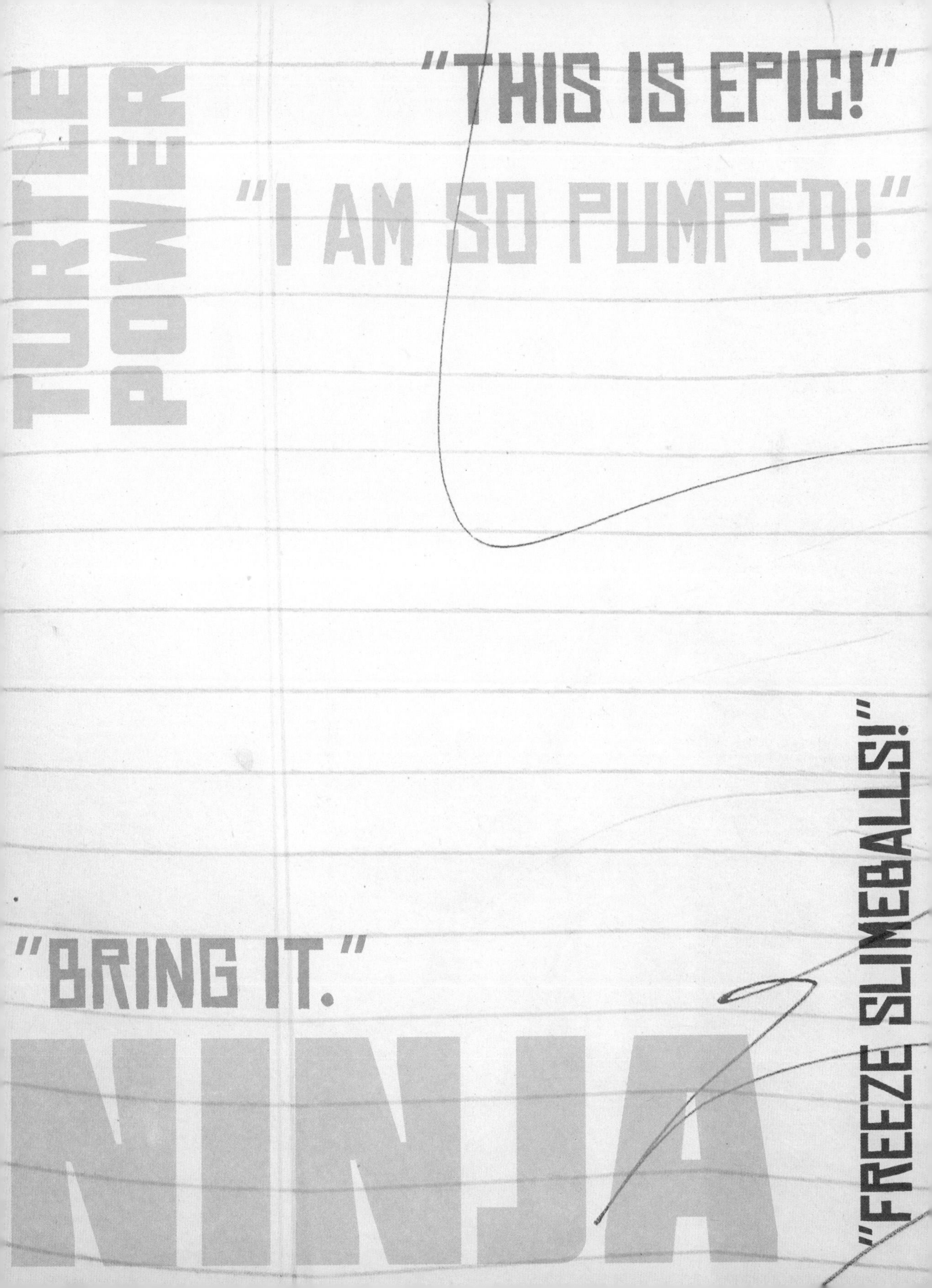
TURTLE
POWER
"THIS IS EPIC!"
"I AM SO PUMPED!"
"BRING IT."
NINJA
"FREEZE SLIMEBALLS!"

WRITE A LIST OF NEW, **TURTLE-POWERED** PIZZA TOPPINGS!
PIZZA
PIZZA

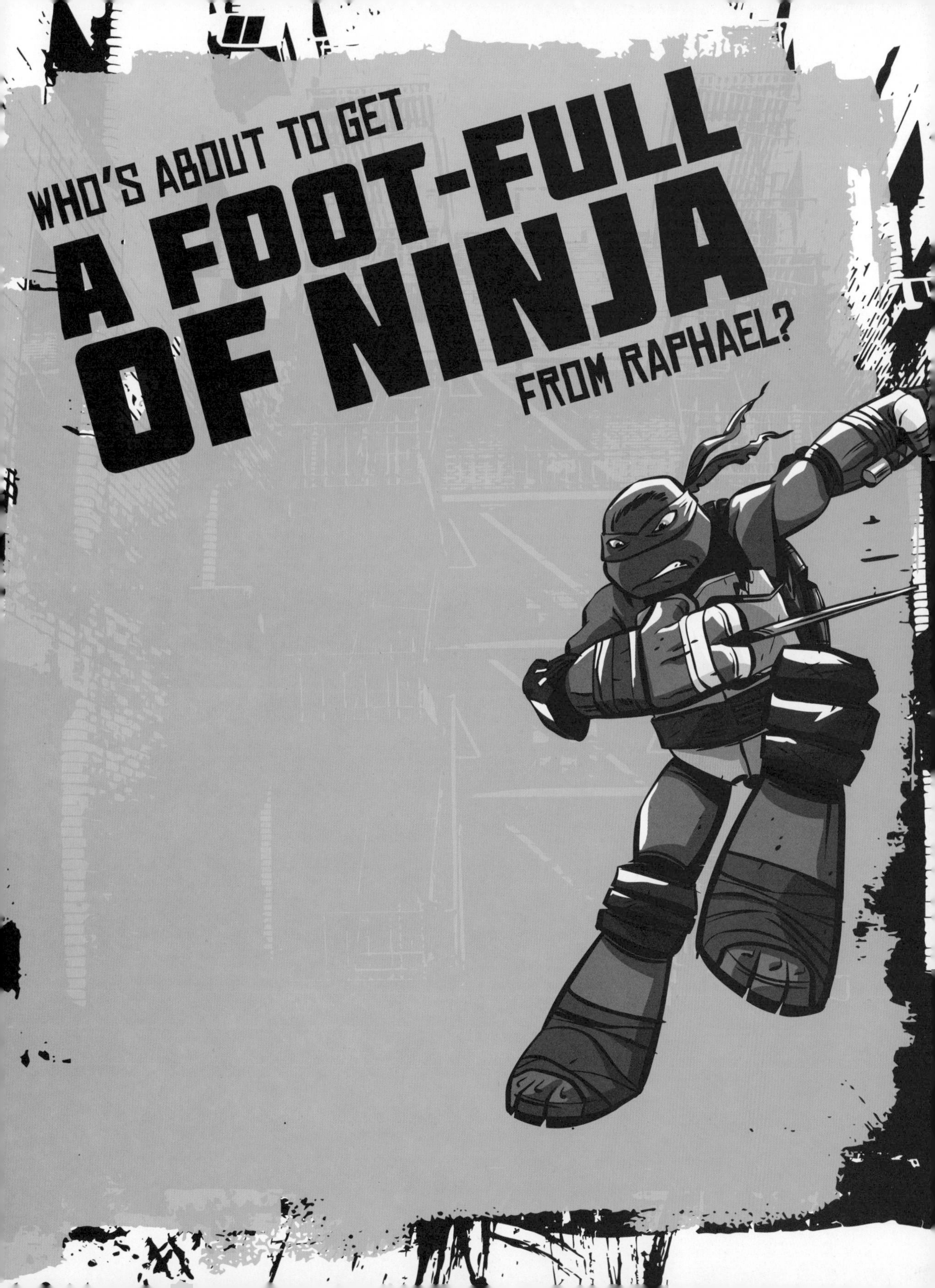
WHO'S ABOUT TO GET
A FOOT-FULL
OF NINJA
FROM RAPHAEL?

HEROES DON'T ASK FOR PERMISSION!
DOODLE WHATEVER TURTLE

PICTURES YOU LIKE ON THESE PAGES.

SPLINTER IS
TRAINING TOUGH TURTLE.
RAPHAEL.
SKETCH AN OPPONENT FOR HIM!

THE TURTLES
WORK AS A TEAM.
PICK THREE FRIENDS AND DRAW
YOUR NINJA TEAM.

DOODLE
. . . A PICTURE OF YOUR TOP TURTLE
WITHOUT TAKING YOUR PENCIL OFF THE PAGE!

TURTLES HAVE TO BE BATTLE-READY SUPER-QUICK!

DRAW YOURSELF IN JUST ONE MINUTE.

WHAT'S JUST SENT MIKEY
FLYING THROUGH THE AIR?

DONNIE IS TOTALLY PUMPED
FOR ACTION. WHAT GETS YOU PUMPED?

DRAW IT!

LEO
1
2
3
4
5
6
A
B
C
D
E
F
IS IN TRAINING

CAN YOU COPY HIS PICTURE, WITH STRICT ATTENTION TO DETAIL?

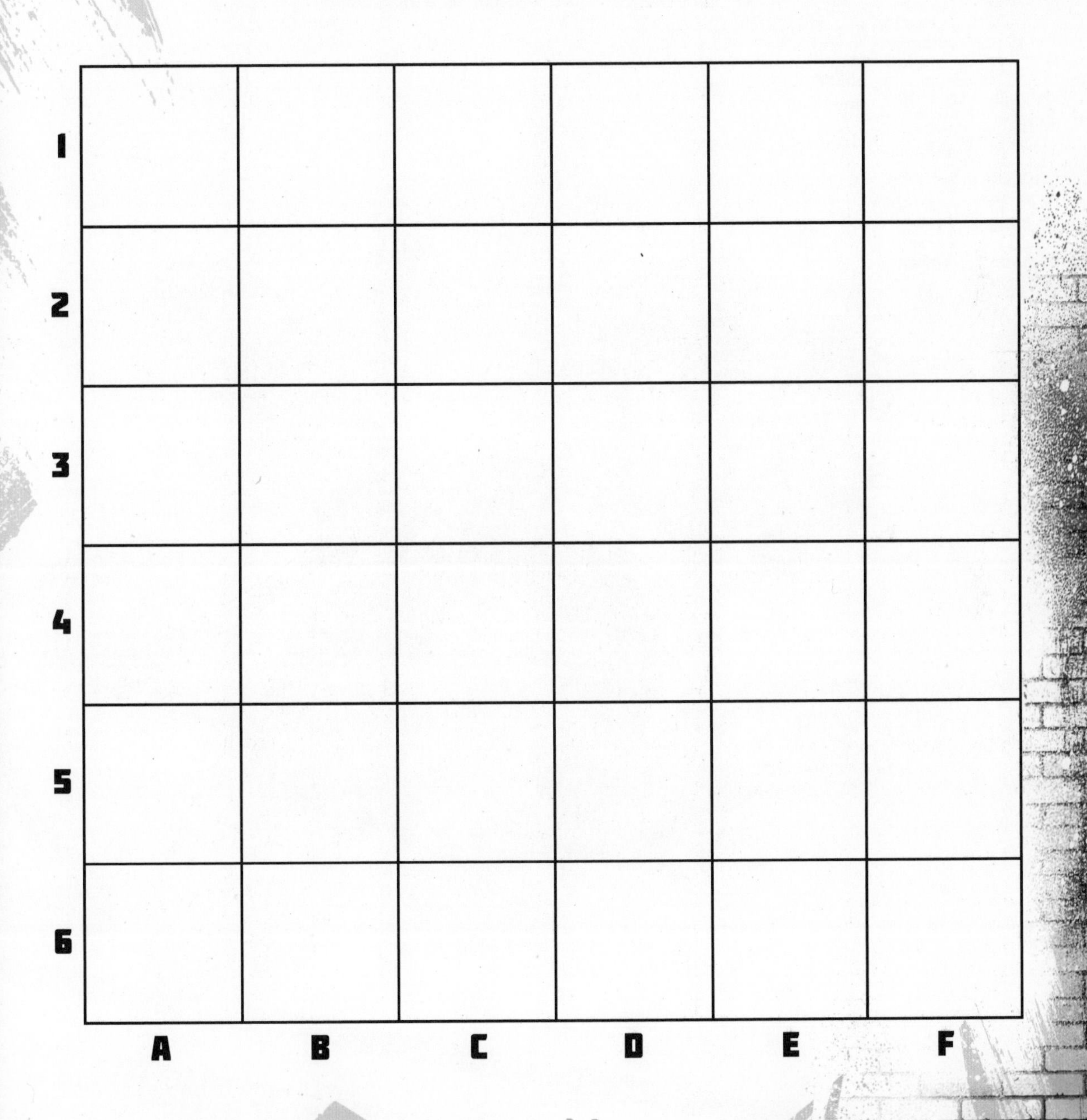

MICHELANGELO
IS THE JOKER OF
THE GROUP.
DRAW A PICTURE OF THE BEST
PRANK YOU'VE EVER PLAYED!

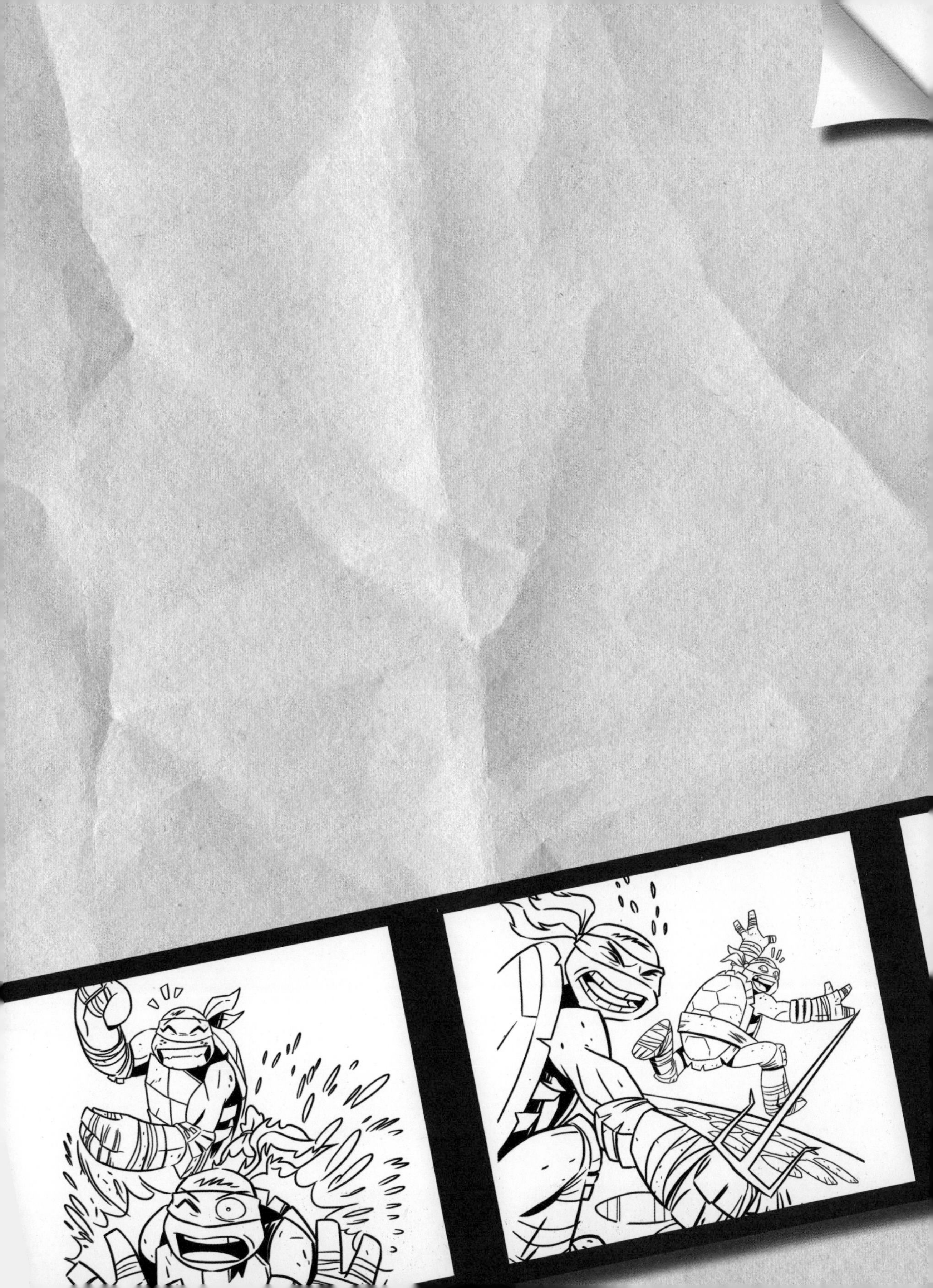

FILL THESE PAGES WITH TURTLE
GADGET IDEAS!

MINI WEAPONS...

REMOTE CONTROLS...

WALKIE TALKIES...

NUNCHUCKS

DRAW SPLINTER DOING AN ULTIMATE NINJA MOVE!

SHRED-HEAD

WANTS SOME TURTLE SOUP!
WHAT'S MADE HIM SO MAD?

SKETCH SHREDDER'S DARK LAIR AROUND HIM.

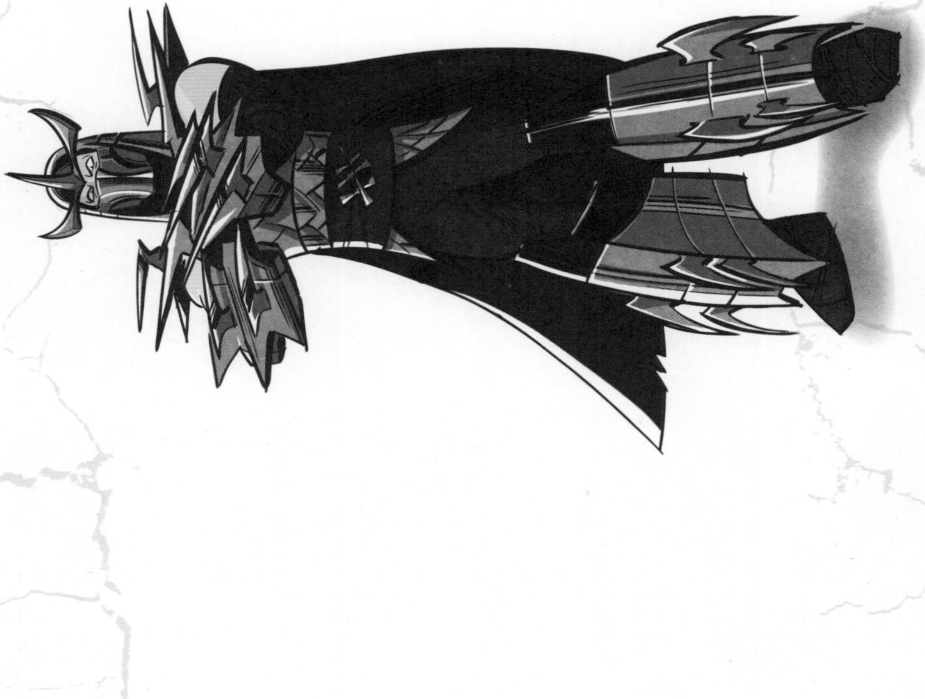

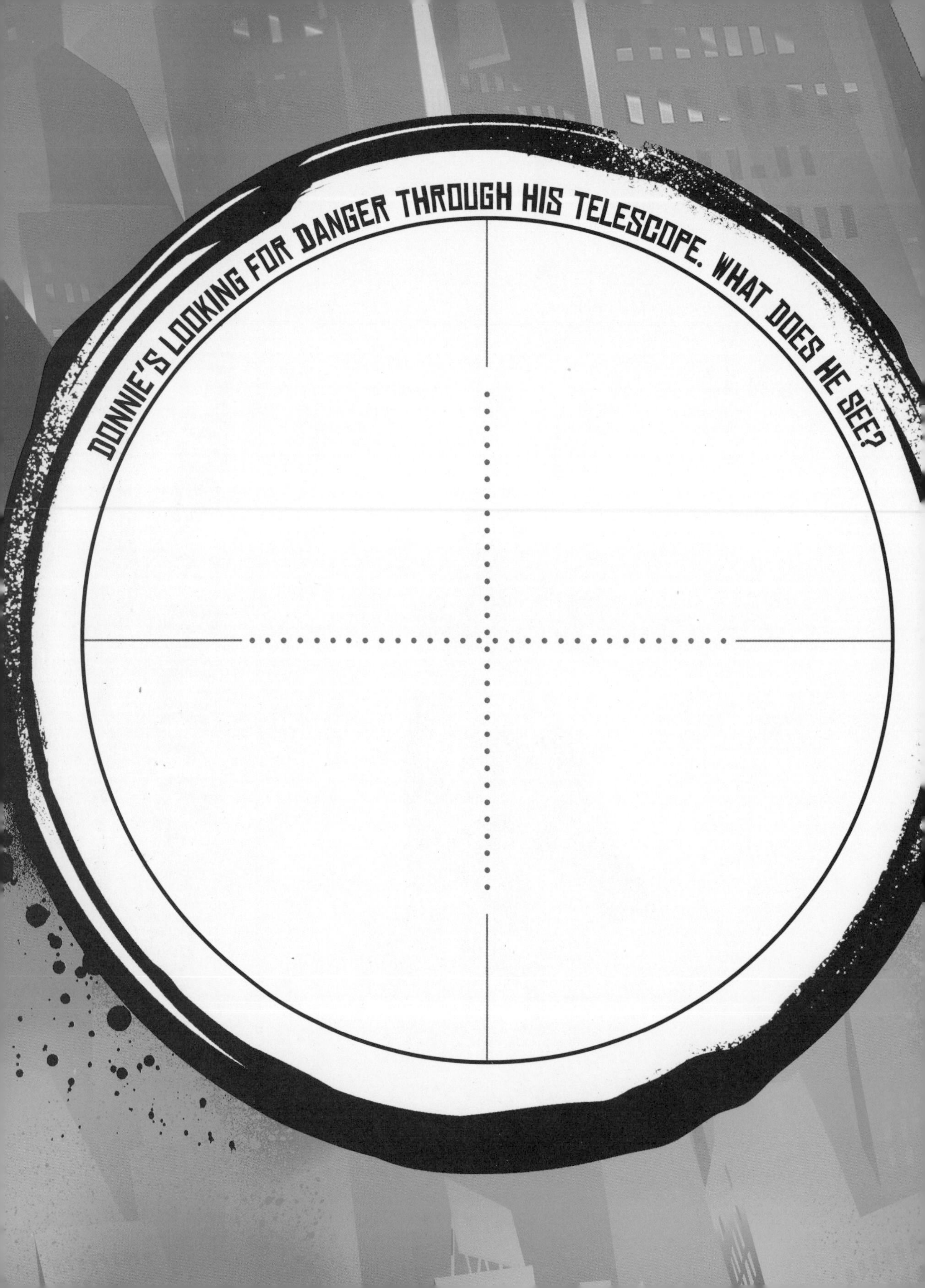
DONNIE'S LOOKING FOR DANGER THROUGH HIS TELESCOPE. WHAT DOES HE SEE?

IMAGINE IF SHREDDER AND SPLINTER HAD A FIGHT.

DRAW WHAT MIGHT HAPPEN!

THE TURTLES ARE BEING ATTACKED BY BALLS OF DOOM FROM ABOVE! DRAW THE BALLS OF DOOM.

THE KRAANG

PLAN TO INFECT THE CITY WITH MUTAGEN!

HOW WILL THEY DO IT? WHEN? WHERE?

SKETCH HOW THE TURTLES WILL STOP THEM!

SPLINTER ALWAYS HAS SOMETHING WISE TO SAY.
WHAT'S THE BEST ADVICE YOU'VE EVER HAD?
WRITE IT IN THE BUBBLES.

RAPHAEL HAS A PET TURTLE CALLED SPIKE.
DRAW YOUR OWN AWESOME PET OR THE ONE YOU WISH YOU HAD.

NYC

ARE YOU GOOD AT INVENTING, LIKE DONNIE?

WHAT WOULD YOU CREATE FROM A MANHOLE COVER, A DROID ARM, AND A BO STAFF?

RAPHAEL USES HIS SAI FOR FIGHTING . . . AND EATING!

DRAW HIS SAI HERE.

THE FOOT CLAN SOLDIERS ARE FIGHTING THE TURTLES. DRAW ONE SOLDIER ABOUT TO BE SHELL-SHOCKED!

DECORATE EACH TURTLE'S SHELL . . .

MICHELANGELO

...TO MATCH THEIR PERSONALITY!

DONATELLO

MIKEY IS FULL OF SURPRISES!

WHAT HAS HE JUST DONE TO SHOCK THE OTHER TURTLES?

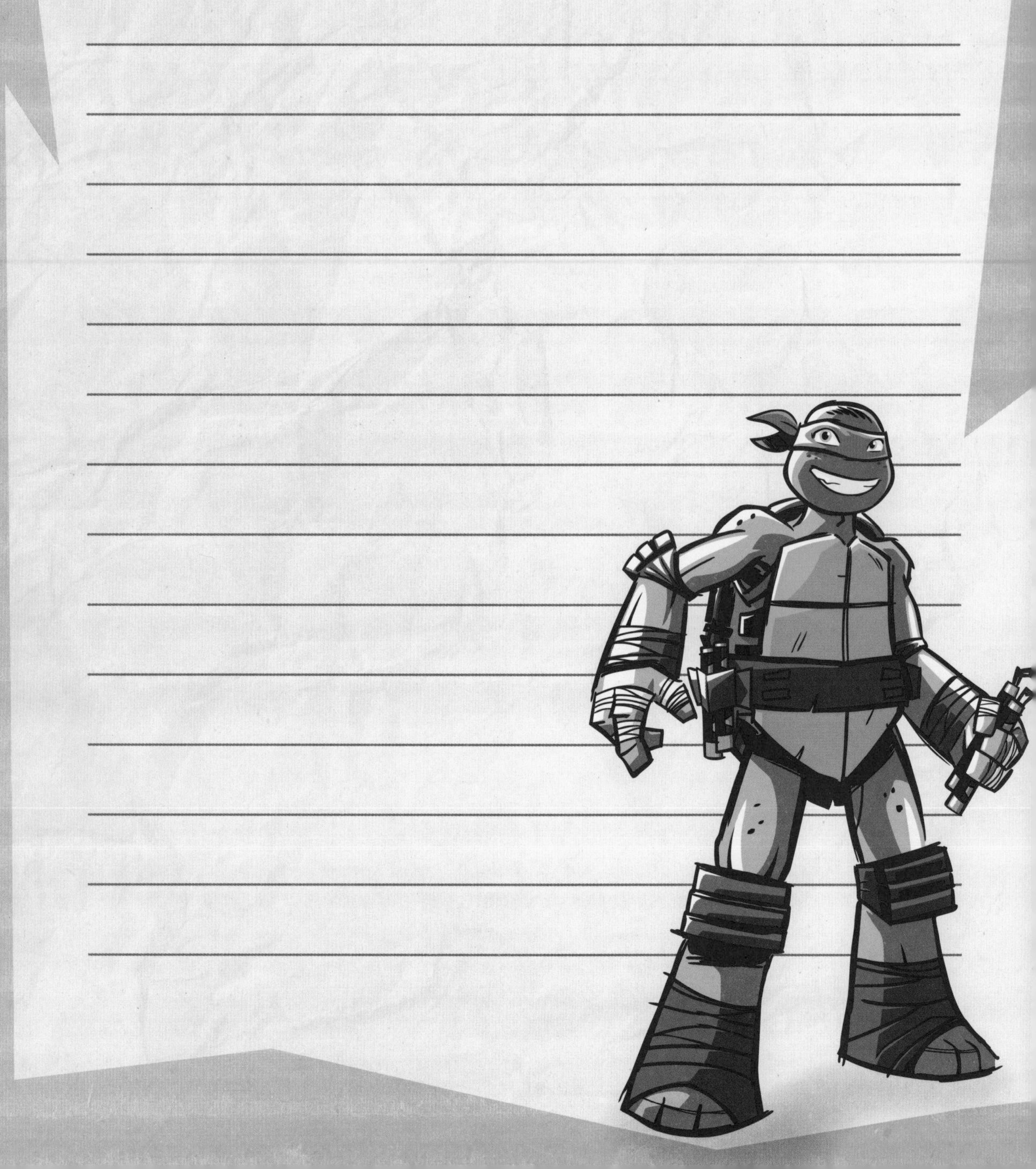

LEO'S HERO IS CAPTAIN RYAN FROM *SPACE HEROES*. DRAW YOUR ULTIMATE HERO!

MIKEY IS OBSESSED!
DRAW YOURSELF AND YOUR FRIEN
AS VIDEOGAME CHARACTERS.

DELIVER A SWINGING
NUNCHUCK SMACKDOWN!
ADD MIKEY'S WEAPON
TO HIS PICTURE.

GIVE THIS SKATEBOARD AN AWESOME TURTLE DESIGN!

CHECK THIS OUT!

CREATE YOUR OWN TURTLE GRAFFITI WITH
YOUR FAVORITE REPTILE CATCHPHRASE.

DRAW FIVE THINGS THAT YOU THINK **SHREDDER** COULDN'T SWIPE THROUGH WITH HIS STEEL SLASHERS!

TWO KATANA ARE BETTER THAN ONE.

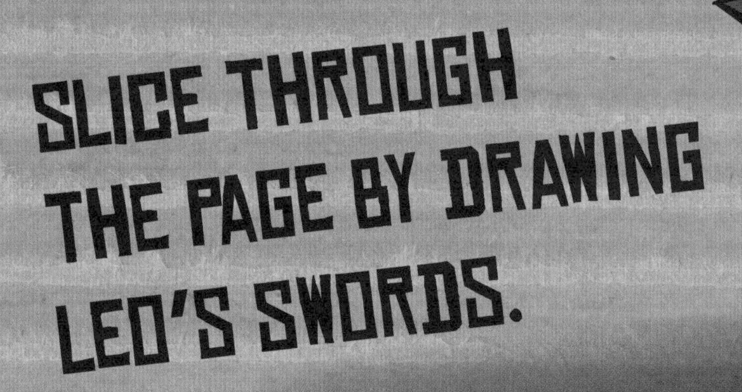

SLICE THROUGH
THE PAGE BY DRAWING
LEO'S SWORDS.

THE TURTLES NEED A NEW GADGET TO FOLLOW APRIL.

CAN YOU HELP DONNIE INVENT A TRACKER?

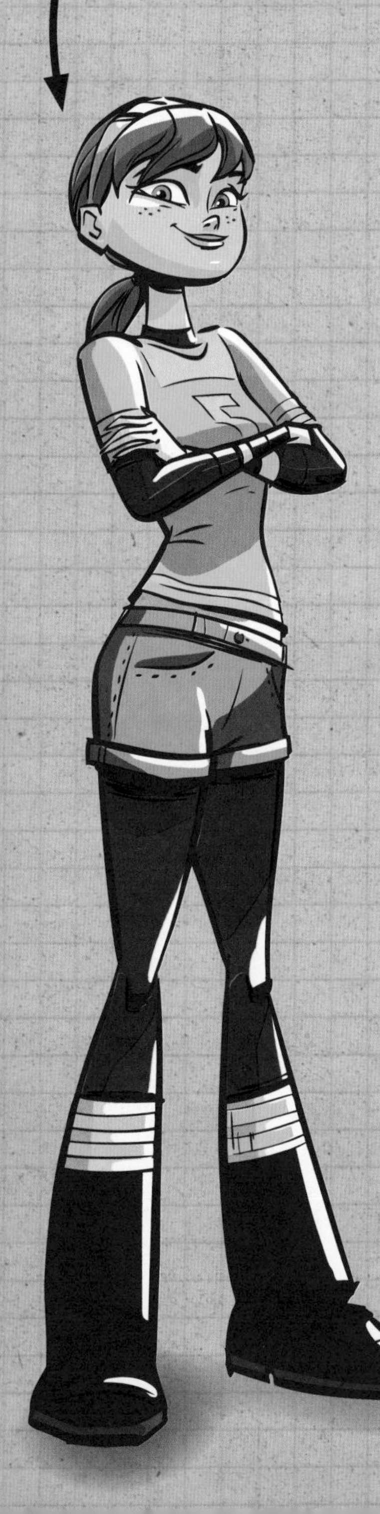

'CHUCK THIS OUT!

WHAT'S MIKEY ABOUT TO TAKE OUT WITH HIS WEAPON?

WHAT MIGHT HAPPEN IF THE TURTLES WENT OUT IN THE DAYTIME?
SKETCH IT HERE.

THE KRAANG ARE ATTACKING!
SKETCH THE TURTLES
PREPARING TO FIGHT.

SHREDDER HAS SOME PRETTY SHARP SKILLS! ADD MORE KNIVES TO HIS DEADLY ARMOR.

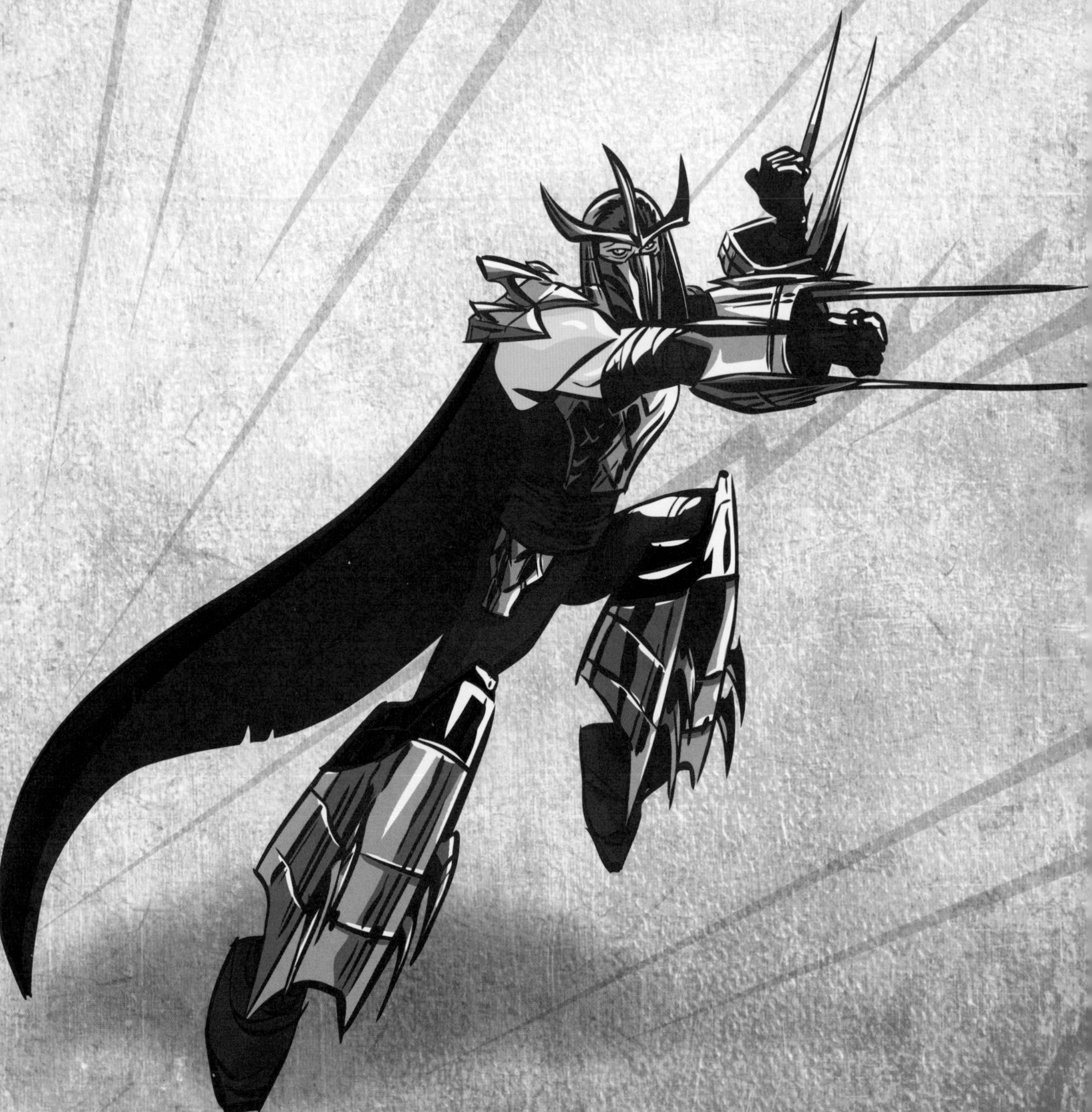

THE TURTLES HAVE SPOTTED THE KRAANG WITH A

"SUB-SPACIAL ENDO-PARTICLE DISRUPTOR"

WHAT DOES IT LOOK LIKE?

CLUE: IT MAKES THINGS GO **BOOM!**

HAI SENSEI!

SKETCH THE TURTLES' BEST NINJA MOVES!

YOU SPEND THE DAY WITH THE TURTLES. WHAT HAPPENS . . . ?

AN ARMY OF KRAANGDROIDS ARE COMING THROUGH THE SEWERS!

ADD MORE PIPES TO STOP THEM FROM REACHING THE TURTLES.

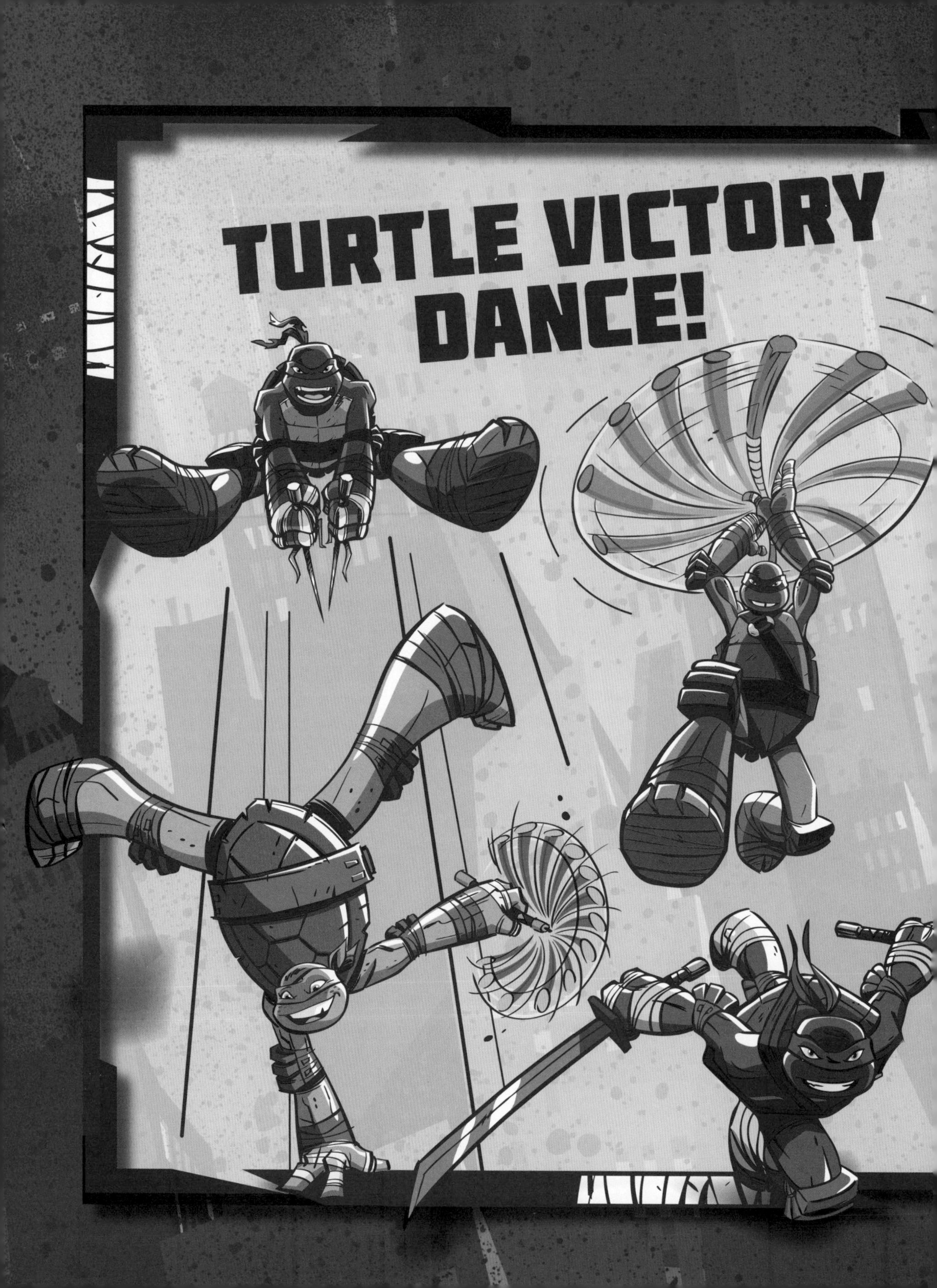
TURTLE VICTORY DANCE!

DRAW THE PERFECT WINNERS' MOVES, NINJA STYLE!

THIS IS TO CERFIFY THAT

....

HAS COMPLETED THE NINJA CREATIVITY CHALLENGE!

YOU ARE A TURTLES MASTER SKETCHER! COMPLETE YOUR OWN SPECIAL CERTIFICATE TO FINISH.